Mississippi Native Americans

A Kid's Look at Our State's Chiefs, Tribes, Reservations, Powwows, Lore, and More From The Past and the Present

By Carole Marsh

Native American Heritage™

Graphic Design: Lynette Rowe • Cover Design: Victoria DeJoy

Native American Heritage™

Carole Marsh Books

Published by
Gallopade International™
800-536-2GET
www.gallopade.com

Gallopade is proud to be a member of these educational organizations and associations:

The National School Supply and Equipment Association (NSSEA)
American Booksellers Association (ABA)
Virginia Educational Media Association (VEMA)
Association of Partners for Public Lands (APPL)
Museum Store Association (MSA)
National Association for Gifted Children (NAGC)
Publishers Marketing Association (PMA)
International Reading Association (IRA)
Association of African American Museums (AAAM)

Native American Heritage™ Series

Native American
Big Activity Book

Native American
Biographies

Native American
Coloring Book

Native American
Heritage Book

Native American
Timeline

Mississippi State Stuff™

- My First Pocket Guide: Mississippi
- My First Book About Mississippi
- Mississippi Coloring Book
- The Big Mississippi Reproducible Activity Book
- Jeopardy: Answers & Questions About Our State
- Mississippi "Jography!": A Fun Run Through Our State
- Mississippi Gamebooks
- Mississippi Bingo Games
- Mississippi Illustrated Timelines
- Mississippi Project Books
- Mississippi Bulletin Board Set
- Mississippi PosterMap
- Mississippi Stickers
- Let's Discover Mississippi! CD-ROM

Word from the Author

Hello!

I hope you are as interested in North America's wonderful Indian heritage as I am!

Like most kids, I grew up thinking of Indians as the other half of Cowboys. Today, of course, we are getting a much clearer and more accurate picture of what the first peoples on our land were all about. These "facts" are much more fascinating than anything Hollywood can make up. And you probably won't find much of this information in your history textbook!

I am 1/16 Cherokee. This is something I am very proud of and happy about. My grandmother was 1/4 Cherokee. She had tan skin, long gray hair and a very Indian look – especially if I did something bad! Her maiden name was Carrie Corn. Of course, when she got married, she took her husband's name, so it was many years before I learned to appreciate the significance of my native heritage.

Today, I'm trying to make up for lost time by exploring my roots as deeply as I can. One of the most interesting things I've learned is how fascinating all of the Indian tribes are – in the past, the present and future!

As you read about "your" Indians, remember that all native peoples were part of an ever-changing network of time, ideas, power and luck — good and bad. This is certainly a history that is not "dead," but continues to change – often right outside our own back doors! – all the time.

Carole Marsh

She-Who-Writes

PS: Many references show different spellings for the same word. I have tried to select the most common spelling for the time period described. I would not want to be in an Indian spelling bee!

A is for . . .

Achougoula

From the Choctaw word ashunga which means pipe. A Natchez village of pipe people around 1699.

Awl

An Indian's "needle." Often made from wood, thorns, bone, or metal, it was used to punch holes in skins so they could be sewn together.

Adze

An Indian woodworking tool used to cut, scrape, or gouge; often used to hollow dugout canoes. Blades were made of stone, shell, bone or copper.

Archaeology

At the Cobb Institute of Archaeology at Mississippi State University you can see exhibits of Indian materials from the Mississippi culture.

Agriculture

Early Mississippi Indians slowly learned to farm. Corn or maize was a staple crop. They used tools like stone axes to clear trees and bowls to grind corn.

Altar

A platform made of rocks or animal skulls; some had bowls, feathers, rattles, or skins on them. Indians prayed at these altars for things like good crops or expert hunting skills.

Arrow

A long, slender shaft made of reed, cane, or wood; pointed tip was attached to one end and split feathers to the other. Feathers helped the arrows fly straight.

Aborigine

A member of the earliest known population of a region.

Arrowhead

The pointed tip of an arrow, made of bone, antler, wood, or iron. Some tips had barbs that would embed themselves in flesh. These barbs made it difficult for an enemy to remove the arrowhead from a wound.

Ayanabi

Choctaw town on Yannubbee Creek where Creeks and Choctaws met to make peace in the early 18th century.

B is for . . .

Boat Stones

Stone objects found in Mississippi believed to have been charms worn by Indians around the neck.

Band

A subdivision of an Indian tribe. In earlier times, a band was sometimes created when part of a tribe split off from the main group. The band also chose new leadership.

Bayogoula

Choctaw word for "the bayou people." Most of this tribe was killed either in battle or by a 1721 smallpox epidemic.

Baskets

Some were woven and others were coiled. Baskets were made from roots, grasses, barks, and other natural materials.

Biloxi

Small Indian tribe that once lived in the lower part of Mississippi. They spoke a completely different language than their neighbors.

Buckskin

Softened, smoke-treated rawhide. Used by Mississippi Indians to make clothes, bags and pouches.

Bow

Made from wood, horn or bone. Mississippi Indian children learned how to use bows. The bowstring was made from animal gut, rawhide or twisted vegetable fibers.

Bogue Chitto

Choctaw Indians that once lived in Neshoba and Kemper Counties; name means "big bayou." Part of the western division of the Choctaw.

Beads

Made of wood, shells, claws, minerals, seeds — you name it! Later, the Mississippi Indians traded with white men for glass beads, used in some of their decorative arts.

C is for . . .

Chief

Leader of a tribe. Different titles meant different things. Some members were made chief because they owned deeds to land. Chieftainship was often inherited, usually from the mother!

Contact Period

What historians call the era in the 1500s when Native Americans first met Europeans. This meeting changed the lifestyle of the Mississippi Indians more than anyone could ever have anticipated!

Chatelaw

Old Chickasaw town; name means "copper town." It was located in northern Mississippi.

Chickasaw

One of the warlike Gulf Coast tribes. They lived in villages and farmed. Their language was widely used for trade along the Mississippi River. Once lived on the Mississippi, Yazoo and Tallahatchie Rivers. Northern Mississippi was the center of their ancestral homelands. Although many migrated west of the Mississippi River due to settlement, they were still removed to Indian Territory in 1837. They became known as one of the "Five Civilized Tribes."

Cabusto

Chickasaw town in northeastern Mississippi as early as the mid-1500s.

Confederacy

A union of different groups of people. A confederacy in Indian culture was a group of tribes that agreed not to fight with each other. They agreed to live peacefully. Sometimes the tribes shared culture and language.

Choctaw Museum of the Southern Indian

Located at Philadelphia; run by the Mississippi Band of the Choctaw. Stresses the cultural community of the tribe. See displays of basketry, costumes, drums and more.

Citizenship

The Indian Citizenship Act of 1924 states all Indians born in the United States are citizens of the United States, and citizens of the states they live in, even though they may live on a reservation. They can vote. They pay most local, state and federal taxes, including sales taxes.

Choctaw

Once one of the largest tribes in the southeast. Were villagers and farmers. Name is said to come from the Spanish word chato, which means flat, for their practice of head-flattening. Today, the Mississippi Band of Choctaw Indians can be found in east-central Mississippi. Their original land holdings granted in 1944 were 15,150 acres divided into 7 sections. Today the tribe has managed to rebound from poverty and has created many jobs, manufacturing operations, and gaming centers.

Clan

A tribal unit. Members are descended from the same ancestor.

Chakchiuma

Indian tribe that once lived in central Mississippi. They were powerful, skilled hunters, and known for their large size. Their name means "red crawfish." Lived in a walled town, and was part of the Chickasaw confederacy in the 1700s.

D is for . . .

Dance

There were Indian dances for every occasion: war, peace, hunting, rain, good harvests, etc. Drums, rattles, and flutes of bone or reed provided the music. Dancers often chanted or sang while performing. Steps were not easy to learn and required consistent practice.

Descendants

The first Mississippi Indians were descendants of primitive hunters who crossed the Bering Strait from Asia to what is now Alaska. At that time, glacial ice still covered most of North America. These people were the true discoverers of the "New World!"

Dancing Rabbit Creek

Here the Choctaw Indians signed a treaty in 1830 trading their land in Mississippi for land they had never seen in Oklahoma. They made this swap only after much pressure was put upon them by the government to do so. By 1832, most of the Choctaw had left.

Dyes

Made of lichens, berries, roots, bark, plants, and other natural materials by Indians in Mississippi. Different colors were used depending on what materials were available and what objects were to be dyed.

Disease

Mississippi Indians had no immunity to the diseases that white explorers, colonists and settlers brought to their lands. These diseases included smallpox, measles, tuberculosis and others, which ravaged the tribes in great epidemics that killed many, and sometimes all, members of a tribe.

Dead

The Choctaw practiced a strange ritual when burying their dead. First they cleaned the bones, then put them in boxes and baskets in bone houses. This was done by older male members of the tribe who had very long fingernails, grown just for this purpose!

Dishes

Made from clay, bark, wood, stone, and other materials, depending on what was available and what food they would be used for.

Dreams

Important in the Indian tradition. It was believed that dreams were the "windows" to the soul. Many thought a person's hidden desires were expressed in dreams.

E is for . . .

Eagle

An animal used in many Indian ceremonies. Eagle feathers attached to war bonnets and shields communicated an Indian's rank in his tribe and what kinds of deeds he had done. Feathers also adorned rattles, pipes, baskets, and prayer sticks.

Ebita Poocola Chitto

Former Choctaw town once located at the head of Straight Creek in Mississippi. The name meant "fountain head" or "big people."

Emerald Mound

Near Natchez; built and occupied between 1250 and 1600 A.D. One of the largest ceremonial mounds in the U.S., covering 8 acres.

Effigy Mound Culture

Built earthen figures of birds, animals or people.

Earrings

Medicine men sometimes pierced male and female ears at special ceremonies. Earrings, which cost parents or relatives a significant amount, symbolized wealth and distinction. The more earrings that an Indian wore, the greater his honor. Some earrings measured 12 inches in length!

Environment

Preserving the environment is important to preserving Native American heritage. For thousands of years, Native American tribes lived completely off the land. Farming, mining, pollution have all had a part in changing native environments.

English

In the 1800s, the U.S. government built boarding schools for Indian children throughout the nation. Children were forced to leave their homes and families to live at these schools. They were required to learn English and not speak their native languages.

Epidemics

Few Indians possessed immunity to the deadly diseases, like smallpox and measles, which European explorers and settlers brought to the New World. As a result, great population loss took place. Sometimes entire tribes became extinct. Epidemics sparked by Hernando De Soto's expedition are estimated to have killed 75% of the native population in the New World.

F is for . . .

Five Civilized Tribes

European settlers dubbed the Seminole, Choctaw, Chickasaw, Creek, and Cherokee the Five Civilized Tribes. After these tribes had been moved to Indian lands west of the Mississippi, they lived peacefully, farmed, and maintained governments similar to the colonial government. These actions made them "civilized" in the settlers' eyes.

Fetish

These small objects were thought to hold the spirit of an animal or a part of nature. A fetish could be an object found in nature, such as bone or wood, or it could be a carved object. The fetish was usually small enough to be carried in a small bag or on a cord. The making and use of a fetish was kept secret by its owner and only shared with the one who inherited it.

Farmers

Many Mississippi Indians, ancient and modern, have farming ways! Even pre-contact Indians tilled and irrigated, raising many important crops. Corn, cotton, beans, squash, melons, sunflowers, gourds, pumpkins and tobacco are all native Indian crops!

Federal Recognition

The United States government's official acknowledgement of a group of Indians as a tribe that is eligible for government benefits, programs and funds.

Fire Drill

A device used by Indians to make fires which consisted of a stick and a piece of wood with a tight hole in it. The stick was twirled rapidly in the hole, creating friction that would ignite shredded grass or wood powder placed nearby to start a fire.

Footwear

Mississippi Indians wore different footwear depending on their tribe and environment. Moccasins were made mostly of animal skin. Sandals were made of rawhide or plant material.

French and Indian War

Broke out in 1745 over boundary lines between New France and the British colonies. The British defeated the French and their Indian allies. A peace treaty in 1763 ended the war, when Canada and most French possessions east of the Mississippi River were given to the English.

G is for . . .

Games

Adults played ball and other games of chance or skill. Indian children spun tops, fought pretend battles, did target-shooting, walked on stilts, played hide and seek, or competed to see who could hold their breath the longest!

Grand Village

Of the Natchez Indians; located near the town of Natchez. A 128-acre National Historic Landmark. Location of the ceremonial mound religious and political center for the Natchez tribe. A museum contains locally-collected artifacts.

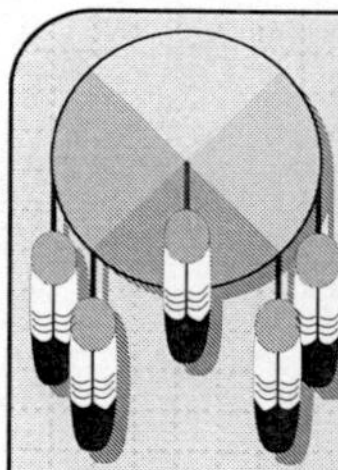

Great Sun

Chief of the Natchez Indians; had life and death power over his subjects, and was similar to a king. When he died, his wife and servants had to give up their lives so that they could go with the Great Sun to the next world.

Gens

Group of related members from different tribes.

Gathering

Native Americans gathered natural materials for food, fuel, baskets, clothing, and housing. American Indians tribes also hunted to meet basic needs. Even though some tribes planted crops, most did some kind of gathering.

Gorgets

Beautiful ornaments hung around the neck or from ears; their significance, if any, is unknown.

Grigras

Small Indian tribe that was protected by the Natchez Indians. Part of the Natchez confederacy in 1720.

Gourds

Hollowed-out shell of a gourd plant's dried fruit which often grew into a specific shape. Indians raised many species of gourds. They were used for spoons, bowls, masks, rattles, and even storage.

Go To These Exciting Indian Events in Our State!

Annual Spring Powwow – April, Gulfport/Rice Pavili; Annual Natchez Powwow – March, Natchez; Annual Chata Inter-tribal Powwow – July, Philadelphia; Annual Choctaw Indian Fair – July, Choctaw; Annual White Buffalo Pow Wow – September, Tupelo.

H is for . . .

Horn and Hooves

Indians used animal horn to make spoons and dishes. Hooves were made into rattles and bird beaks were used for decoration.

Hatchet

A small, short-handled ax, primarily used as a tool, not as a weapon. When settlers moved in, stone hatchets were replaced with iron ones.

Hair

Indians used hair as a textile. Hair from bison, mountain sheep, elk, moose, deer, dog, rabbit, beaver, or even humans were used to weave cloth, make wigs, or stuff pillows, balls, dolls or drumsticks.

Head Flattening

The significance of this Choctaw custom, flattening the heads of young children, remains unknown. Experts say flat heads might have symbolized beauty or higher social standing. Parents laid their babies in hinged cradle boards to press their skulls or against boards with weighted leather strips.

Hunters

Early Indian peoples were hunters who used wooden spears with stone points to kill many kinds of large mammals that are extinct today, such as mammoths and mastodons!

Head of Curls or Curly Head

Well-known Indian chief of the Mississippi Chippewa. Died in 1825.

Horses

Spaniards brought the horse to America. At first, Indians were afraid of the horse or thought it was sacred. Later, Indians "broke" horses gently, often "hypnotizing" them with a blanket. Horses were used for transportation, trade, barter or payment. Some Indians ate horse meat in hopes of gaining the animal's power.

Hykehah

Former Chickasaw town located near Pontotoc County.

Help!

The name of the town of Cushtusha in Mississippi meant "fleas are there" in the Choctaw language. It was a notable Choctaw town.

I is for . . .

Inkillis Tamaha

Choctaw town located in Jasper County. Name means "English town." Given because it was a center for the distribution of property by the English.

Indian Reservation

A tract of land set aside by a government for Indians to live on.

Indian Removal Act of 1830

This federal act gave President Andrew Jackson the power to relocate tribes east of the Mississippi to an "Indian Territory." The forced removal of the southeast Indians later became known as the "Trail of Tears."

Independence

Native American tribes are sovereign nations. That means they are independent. Some even issue their own passports! However, Native Americans are also considered citizens of the United States and enjoy all the rights and privileges of U.S. citizens.

Indian Nation

The "Five Civilized Tribes" removed to Indian Territory were the Choctaw, Chickasaw, Creek, Seminole, and Cherokee. Each of these tribes was a part of the "Indian Nation," as the Indian Territory was called historically. Today, each of these tribes is a nation by itself. The old "Indian Nation" also included other tribes in the Gulf of Mexico states.

Indian

In 1493, Christopher Columbus called the native people he met in North America "Indians" because he mistakenly believed he had sailed to India! Today, this term includes the aborigines of North and South America.

Indian Ladder

Indians made ladders by trimming branches off a tree. Some were left at consistent intervals to provide steps.

Indian Tribes in Mississippi

At one time or another, these tribes have lived in the state of Mississippi:
Biloxi, Chakchiuma, Chickasaw, Chitimachas, Choctaw, Grigras, Houmas, Natchez, Tunica, Yazoo

J is for . . .

Just So You Know . . .

Today you can find many Mississippi Indians that follow some traditional ways. But there are also many who are entrepreneurs, doctors, lawyers, educators and even politicians! If you visit a reservation or cultural event, make sure you know visitor etiquette. Often dances are religious ceremonies and should be observed as such; religious dances should not be applauded. Photography, videotaping and drawing are all important issues - check with the tribe or individual before any is started.

Jesuits

Roman Catholic priests called Jesuits were among the first to meet and live with the North American Indians. Their writings, sent back to Europe, serve as one of today's best references to early Indian life.

Justice?

For hundreds of years, Native Americans have not received justice from federal and state governments. Native Americans have had nearly all their land taken away. Native Americans still have to fight for their rights in courts across the land.

Judicial Termination

Modern term to describe current efforts by various U.S. government agencies and officials (especially the judicial system) to legally decrease the sovereignty of independent Indian tribes.

Just In Time!

The Indian Arts and Crafts Act of 1990 makes it against the law to pretend that an item has been made by Native Americans if it is really not. It is illegal to offer or display for sale, or sell any art or craft product in a way that falsely suggests it is Indian produced.

Jerked Meat

Thin strips of buffalo, elk, deer or other animal meat which is dried on racks in the sun; also called "jerky."

K is for . . .

Kaffetalaya

Choctaw Indian town on Owl Creek in Neshoba County.

Kill Site

An archaeological site where remains of many animals have been found along with human artifacts. Many kill sites have been useful to scientists in learning how ancient American Indians lived.

Killed Pottery

Pottery placed in a grave as an offering to the dead person was called killed pottery. A hole was formed in its base during creation. Often broken pottery was placed in a grave because Indians believed the spirit of the dead person would then be released and could travel.

Knife

Made from various materials such as bone, reed, stone, wood, antler, shell, metal, or animal teeth (bear, beaver, etc.), knives were used as weapons but also creative handiwork.

Knowledge

Knowledge is power. Native Americans shared knowledge with the first European settlers. Native Americans showed settlers how to plant crops, which plants were safe to eat, and other knowledge about the land.

Knots

Tied on bowstrings, spearhead and arrowhead lashings, snowshoes, and other items, knots were sometimes used to keep track of the days like a calendar—each knot equaled 1 day.

L is for . . .

Linguistic Families

There are 56 related groups of American Indian languages. A few of these speech families include Iroquoian, Algonquian, Siouan, Muskogean, Athapascan, and Wakashan.

Leggings

Both men and women wore cloth or skin covering, which were often decorated with quills, beads, or painted designs, for their legs.

Lost Tribes of Israel

This historic theory has been floating around since 721 BC. The 10 lost tribes of Israel are supposedly groups of people gathered together by Sargon, the King of Assyria. Some say he cast out 10 of the 12 tribes of Israel. Many have tried to prove that the American Indians are these missing tribes!

Long Hairs

Unlike other southeast Indians, Choctaw men who wore their hair quite long. This name was given to them by their neighbors.

Lodge

The term for a type of Indian house that was usually a permanent dwelling. The population of a tribe was often estimated by its number of lodges.

Land Loss

Native Americans lost their land in many ways. Conflicts with other tribes, colonization, European settlement, treaties, and removal took away Indian lands.

Lance

Spear used for hunting and war. The hunting lance had a short shaft and a broad, heavy head. The war lance was light and had a long shaft.

Lacrosse

The French named this popular Indian game played with webbed sticks and a ball. Indians of different regions of the country played slightly different versions of the game, but it was an important part of culture to all Indians. Southeastern Indians sometimes played the game to settle land disputes between tribes, sometimes up to 100 points. The men's games were followed by the women's games.

Lariat

These throw ropes made of rawhide, buffalo hair, or horsehair sometimes measured up to 20 feet long!

M is for . . .

Maize

Also called Indian Corn. Known as a "cereal" plant because it probably began as some form of grass. The Indians in our state figured out every possible way to use corn as a food. The only thing the white man added was the creation of "corn flakes!"

Mississippi Mounds

Unlike Indian mounds built in other parts of the United States. They were not burial places, but shrines for worship of the sun.

Mingos

What the Chickasaw Indian chiefs were called.

Mississippi Culture

Constructed mounds as religious shrines. Gathered shellfish, nuts, berries and wild plants for food. Also hunted and fished. Built huts of poles and branches, tanned animal skins and wove baskets. Traded their goods for copper ornaments and tools made by other Indians.

Moccasins

Indian shoes made of animal skin.

Medicine Man

A person who got the power to heal the sick through a secret means, usually from a dream or visions.

Mississippi River

Important to early Indian trade. Our state's Indians traded with Native Americans as far north as Lake Michigan. The name of this river came from the Algonquian words *misi* or great and *sipi* or river.

N is for . . .

Nomadic

A way of life in which people frequently moved from one location to another in search of food. "Seminomadic" people had permanent villages, but left them in certain seasons to hunt, fish, or gather wild plant foods.

Natchez Trace

In 1801, Choctaw and Chickasaw representatives gave the United States permission to build a road from Nashville, Tennessee to Natchez, Mississippi. This narrow path followed routes long used by Indians.

Nation

There are many Indian nations located within the United States, such as the Natchez Nation. Indian nations are called nations because their governments and laws are independent of and separate from the U.S. government. The federal government must have "government to government" relations with these Indian nations, just as it would with foreign nations, like England or Spain.

Names

Indian names were often changed during one's lifetime. These names could be derived from events that happened during the person's birth, childhood, adolescence, war service, or retirement from active tribal life. Some names came from dreams, some were inherited, and sometimes names were stolen or taken in revenge. Today some Indians maintain old, traditional Indian names, while others take modern names. Since settlers often did not read or write Indian languages, they recorded Indian names phonetically (as they "sounded"). Thus Indian names were often misspelled.

November

In 1990, President George Bush approved a joint resolution designating November 1990 "National American Indian Heritage Month." Similar proclamations have been issued each year since 1994.

Natchez

These Indians may have been direct descendants of early temple builders. They had a complex and highly organized society, including organized religion, a caste system, and a system of government that resembled a monarchy. Known for building mounds as temple bases. Also had elaborate death rituals.

Nanih Waiya Mound and Village

Located near Philadelphia; revered in Choctaw legend as the birthplace of the tribe. Also known as Mother Mound.

O is for . . .

Old Bones

No one knows for sure when the first people came to North America, but scientists have dated bones and artifacts discovered at Clovis, New Mexico around 11,200 years old. Testing on a skeleton found on the Channel Islands, off the coast of California showed they were about 13,000 years old. And, evidence of human habitation in southern New Mexico suggests that people may have been there as far back as 38,000 years ago.

Oony

Choctaw town located where Pinkney Mill in Newton County is today.

Origins

Some scientists believe that Native Americans actually came across a land bridge between Asia and North America. They say that during an ice age thousands of years ago, the water level was much lower and people could have walked between the two continents.

Oil

Indians extracted oil from the many layers of fat that came with fresh bear meat. The fat was boiled down in earthen pots to produce the oil, which was stored in gourds and pots. The oil was used for cooking and even beautifying the body! Indians would mix red pigment with the oil, add the fragrances of cinnamon and sassafras, and rub it all over their bodies.

Old Spanish Fort and Museum

Pascagoula; see Indian artifacts, tools and implements plus maps showing Indian settlements before 1700.

Orators

Many Indian leaders were excellent public speakers. Powerful and dramatic speakers were vital to leaders who wanted to influence their tribe. Watch for famous Indian quotations in literature and textbooks!

Office of Indian Education Programs

This is a service organization devoted to providing quality education opportunities for American Indian people. Established in the latter part of the nineteenth century to carry out the federal government's education commitment to Indian tribes, it has become the only national education system for American Indian children and adults.

P is for . . .

Powwow

The original form of the word meant "medicine man." Medicine men would often use noise motion and confusion to scare away harmful spirits and cure people. It was also a gathering to talk about political matters. Today, the powwow is an event where Indians gather to sing, perform ceremonial dances, and share cultural pride and traditions.

Pearls

Southeastern Indians used pearls for decoration and in burial ceremonies. Hernando de Soto dug up many Indian graves to steal the pearls that had been buried there.

Plates

Notched stone plates found in Mississippi that may have been used to grind paint pigments. Some had intricate designs of birds, snakes and other forms of life.

Paint

Indians used many natural materials to make paint, like clay mixed with oil or grease. Yellow "paint" was made with the gall bladder of a buffalo! Why did they paint their faces or bodies? Indians used paint to look scary or beautiful, to disguise themselves, or to protect their skin from sunburn or insect bites. Indians often applied red paint because it symbolized strength and success. That is why settlers often referred to the Indians as Red Men.

Pontotoc

Chickasaw settlement that today is Pontotoc, Mississippi.

Pemmican

Indian food made of animal meat, which was dried in the sun, pounded together with fat and berries. The mixture was packed into skin bags and used primarily while on the trail.

Papoose

An American Indian infant aged between birth and one year is called a papoose. This word also refers to the way infants were bundled and carried by its mother. A papoose spent most of his or her days snugly wrapped in a kind of cradle made of skins or bark and a wooden frame that hung on the mother's back. This sturdy frame also allowed a mother to lean her papoose against a tree or rock within sight as she worked.

Picture History

Some Indians kept a record of time and important events by painting or drawing pictures or symbols on skin, bark, or stone.

Pottery

Indian pottery was made from built-up spirals of clay that were molded or paddled, or a combination of the two methods. Most pottery served as cooking vessels.

Q is for . . .

Quillwork

Indians used the quills of porcupine or birds to make a type of embroidery. Quills were dyed with juice from berries and other materials. When they were ready to be used, the quills were either mashed with teeth or softened with hot water and flattened with rocks. The quills were then laced into moccasins, shirts, pipe covers, and other items. Beads which Indians received by trading with settlers eventually replaced quillwork.

Quality

Native American arts and crafts are known for their excellent craftsmanship and striking designs. This work is often influenced by things found in nature especially plants and animals.

Quiver

Case used to hold arrows; made of woven plant materials or animal skins.

Quarry Site

A location where Indians went for workable stone such as flint and made stone tools.

Quirt

A short riding whip with a wood, bone, or horn handle.

R is for . . .

Rain Dancing

The rain dance ceremony, performed to encourage rainfall, was common among Indian religions because good weather is vital for a successful harvest. Rainmakers were in tune with nature; there are actual reported cases of Indians producing or preventing rain!

Roots

Indians used plant roots for food, medicine, dye, baskets, cloth, rope, salt, flavoring, and just to chew!

Rattles

Indians of Mississippi made rattles from bird beaks, animal hooves, bones, pods, seashells, turtle shells and other animal parts. The rattles are used in ceremonies.

Revolt!

The Natchez Revolt was started by Sieur Chépart, a newly-appointed governor of Louisiana. In 1729, he decided that he wanted the site of the Natchez Great Village seized, to later become his own plantation. The Great Sun, angered by the order to evacuate, plotted a revolt. While the initial attacks were successful and Chépart was killed, the Indians were later overcome by French armies. The armies received help from the Tunica and Choctaw, defeating and dispersing the tribe.

Rawhide

Untanned animal hide. The "green" hide was stretched on the ground or over a frame. Flesh and fat were removed. The skin was dried, washed, then buried with wood ashes which made the hair come off. Used by the Mississippi Indian to make drumheads, lash lodge poles, mend broken objects and in many other ways.

Reservations

The U.S. government set aside, or "reserved," land for the Indians. These reservations originally served as a sort of prison during the beginning stages of Indian removal. At that time, reservations provided the government with some control over Indian activity and residency. This land was usually considerably less desirable land than the Indians' native territories. Today's reservations are lands that are tribally held, yet protected by the government.

Removal

The U.S. government policy of the 1830s-1850s that removed Indians from their native lands to new lands, primarily west of the Mississippi River.

S is for . . .

Sign Language

A way for Indians to communicate with others from a tribe whose language they did not speak.

Shaman

Medicine man and spiritual leader who was supposed to have special healing power from another world.

Secret Societies

Indians had secret groups, usually organized for religious or ceremonial reasons. Each society had a purpose, such as to cure disease.

Shield

A piece of "armor" made of a rawhide-covered frame, which was carried into battle. Shields also could be decorative and religious objects. Many tribes make shields today as an art form!

Sweatlodge

Structure used for ritual purification by sweating from exposure to very hot fires or hot steam from pouring water over hot stones. Also called a sweathouse, for some tribes also doubling as clubhouses.

Stone-boiling

Cooking method by placing preheated stones into cooking vessels.

Sacred Bundles

A group of objects treasured by a tribe. They were well-guarded and often taken into battle. The items were publicly shown only on very important occasions.

Shanhaw

A Choctaw town located in Mississippi.

Stinkards

What Indians in the common class of the Natchez tribe were called.

Schkaha

Former Choctaw village. Located near Philadelphia. Name means "town of sand."

Sachem

The supreme Indian ruler of an area where there are many related tribes.

T is for . . .

Tobacco

A sacred plant early Indians used to make offering to their gods, cure diseases, bring good luck, seal agreements and bind treaties.

Treaties

Written agreements between the U. S. government and the Indians, most of which involved the Indians giving up their native lands.

Trade Language

The Choctaw language was also called the Mobile trade language or the Chickasaw trade language, which was similar.

Totem

The spirit of some natural object (usually an animal) taken by an Indian, tribe or family to guard over them.

Tunica

Tribe of Indians that lived on the lower Yazoo River where it meets the Mississippi River. Villagers who farmed, growing corn, beans, squash, melons, and even sunflowers. Tunica County and Tunica Oldfields are name for them. They also made a fabric from a mulberry plant.

Tomahawk

A club, axe or hammer used to chop wood, drive stakes in the ground or as a weapon.

Tracking

To follow a trail by finding a sign such as a broken blade of grass, a moved stone or moccasin track. Indians learned to trail as children, so that they could find food, track enemies and disguise their own signs.

Teeth

Mississippi Indians hung teeth on cords to make necklaces.

Trail of Tears

Many Choctaw and Chickasaw Indians in Mississippi were forced to join the Cherokee Indians on their march from their homelands in Georgia to Indian Territory in the west. Many of those who went on this winter trek died of disease, starvation or the extreme cold. A few Chickasaw and Choctaw Indians managed to stay in Mississippi for generations; their descendants still live here.

Tribe

A group of Indians with shared culture, history, original territory, ancestry, social organization, and governmental structure. A tribe may contain several bands of Indians.

Thunderbird

A mythological Indian figure, as well as a part of the constellations for many Indians. Thunderbird mythology is mostly different from tribe to tribe, in general either coexisting with ancestors as an actual bird, or appearing as a spiritual nature god. The Thunderbird was good to the people in either case. Much mythology ties the thunderbird with thunder, lightning and storms.

U is for . . .

U.S. Bureau of Indian Affairs

Provides public services such as law enforcement, land records, economic development, and education to Indians. Known for mismanagement and ethical problems.

U.S. Army

Many Native Americans have fought bravely for the United States Army. Many have also given their lives for a country that was not always accepting of them.

Unique

Each and every tribe has its own unique customs, language, and traditions.

U.S. Indian Schools

The Bureau of Indian Affairs operates hundreds of federal schools around the nation. Enrollment of Native American children measures in the thousands!

U.S. Indian Reorganization Act

Passed by Congress in 1934, the act authorized Indian tribes to establish and conduct their own governments, and to form businesses.

U.S. President

Once called Great White Father by Indians.

U.S. Colonists

Called Long Knives or Big Knives by early Indians, who also called English explorers "Coat Men."

U.S. Indian Wars

The U.S. War Department has compiled an official list of "Indian Wars" that occurred in the United States. Over 50 wars were fought between the U.S. and the Indians during the period of 1790-1850.

V is for . . .

Vessels

Indians carried water in special gourds shaped liked bottles, called water vessels.

Village Councils

These were held in the town (council) house and occurred to discuss and decide important matters. Harmony and agreement was essential to tribal unity. Rather than vote on issues, they were discussed until everyone was satisfied. Anyone who wanted to could speak freely. Everyone did not always agree on the outcome, but everyone avoided conflict by pushing their case.

Vegetable Dyes

Indians could not buy color from the store like we can today. Instead, they created many different colors from the things they found on earth like plants, flowers, shrubs, trees, roots, and berries. They made beautiful and unique reds, oranges, yellows, greens, browns, and violets. These dyes were used for baskets, pottery, weaving, body makeup, and clothing.

Very Hungry

There were Indians who here hunters, gatherers and foragers, that often ate whatever they could find! How hungry would you have to be to eat what they sometimes ate: reptiles, larvae, and insects?

Villages

Many Mississippi Indians lived in villages! Villages were formed around different clans or bands within the tribe, but could also contain different clans living together. Villages were usually permanent settlements, although semi-nomadic tribes have been known to migrate between permanent villages.

Vesperic Indians

Indian tribes located in the United States.

W is for . . .

War Bonnet

Special headdress worn into battle, often adorned with feathers.

War Pony

Horse, often painted with colorful paint and ridden into battle.

Witatakali

Choctaw town once located in Neshoba County. Name means "hanging above;" came from the brush roof erected over Choctaw council meeting areas.

War Dance

Indian braves danced this before going into battle. The dance was a way of assembling the braves and getting them to commit to the fight ahead.

Winterville Indian Mounds State Park

Greenville. Site of one of the largest mound groups in the Mississippi valley. Has a museum with artifacts collected at the mound site. See a 5 foot temple mound and 10 smaller mounds.

War of 1812

When war broke out between the United States and Britain, many Choctaw and Chickasaw Indians helped defend our lands. The Choctaw helped General Andrew Jackson crush an uprising of Creek Indians and defeat the British at the Battle of New Orleans.

Whistle

Indians from Mississippi made them from the wing bones of birds. The whistles made the sound of the bird the bones came from! Used to communicate, signal, sound an alarm or even flirt with a maiden!

War Club

A weapon made of stone, bone, or wood in the shape of a club.

World Wars I and II

During these wars, the Choctaw language was used as a secret code by the Army. A Choctaw would be stationed at each end of a field telephone and would transmit messages in his own tongue. The code talker idea was started in World War I by a captain overhearing two Choctaws in his unit talking in their native language while in the field. Inspiration struck, and the use of a handful of Choctaw code talkers in the closing days of the war helped turn the tide for an Allied victory. The code was used again in the European theatre in World War II, and proved unbreakable in both wars.

White Man

Indians generally called them Pale Face, a name the white men themselves suggested!

XYZ are for . . .

Xenophobe

A xenophobe is someone who is afraid of foreign people, their customs and cultures, or foreign things. Many of the first European settlers were afraid of Native American cultures.

Yazoo

Small tribe of Indians that once lived on the lower Yazoo River in Mississippi. In 1729 they attacked the French fort on the river and destroyed it. The meaning of the name is unknown.

Yowani

Choctaw town once located where today's town of Shubuta is in Clarke County. Active around 1764. Indians who lived here were removed to Texas and Louisiana.

Zounds!

Between 1871 and 1913, at least 98 traditional agreements between tribes and the United States were negotiated and 96 of them were ratified by Congress. Each agreement remains as law (unless changed by a later agreement)!

ZZZZZZ...

Shamans and medicine men were not the only people who had access to the spirit world. Indians believed that people could make contact with spirits every night in their dreams! Dreamers could travel back to the time of man's creation or far ahead into their own futures. They also believed that dreams contained warnings or commands from the spirits. Many tribes felt that they had to act out their dreams as soon as they awoke. If an Indian dreamed about bathing, for example, he would run to his neighbors' houses first thing in the morning, and his neighbors would throw kettles full of cold water over him.

Y... Or, "Why?"

1. Why do you think Indian warriors carried charms with them? Some Indian medicines have been scientifically proven to have true healing power and are still used today. Do you think their charms had any real power to help them win battles?
2. Why do you think the American government kept relocating Indians onto reservations and then making the reservations smaller and smaller?
3. Why did Indians use items such as a pipe in ceremonies? What kinds of symbolic objects do we use in ceremonies today?
4. Why and how did Indians use natural materials in creative ways?
5. Many Indian tribes are running successful businesses on their reservations today. There is one industry that many tribes are making a lot of money at. Do you know what this is? Hint: "I'll bet you do!"

Which Famous Native American Am I?

Solve the puzzle!

Word Bank

Black Elk	Crazy Horse	Sitting Bull	Sequoia
Sacajawea	Chief Joseph	Geronimo	Pocahontas

Down

1. This Shoshone woman joined Lewis and Clark as their guide and translator and helped make the expedition a success! Hint: She has 4 "a"s in her name!
4. This man gave the Cherokee their first alphabet so that they could write. Until then, they communicated only by speaking and drawing pictures. Hint: A famous ancient tree also has the same name!
5. He was one of the fiercest of Indian warriors! He fought against white settlers in Arizona and New Mexico to keep his people from being pushed off their lands. Hint: Jump!

Across

2. A legend says that this brave Algonquian woman saved the life of Englishman John Smith. Hint: Disney produced a movie about her.
3. He fought at Little Bighorn when he was only 13! He was also a wise "shaman" who saw visions and could advise people. Hint: Part of his name is an animal with antlers!
6. He was a great Sioux warrior who won the battle against General Custer at Little Bighorn in 1876. Hint: His horse was not crazy!
7. A leader of the Lakota (Sioux) tribe who lived on the Standing Rock Reservation in North Dakota after the battle of Little Bighorn. He tried to make conditions better for his people there, so the U.S. government called him a "troublemaker." Hint: He did not sit all the time!
8. A wise and brave chief of the Nez Percé who tried to bring his people to Canada to escape war. He said, "From where the sun now stands, I will fight no more forever." Hint: His father's name was "Old Joseph."

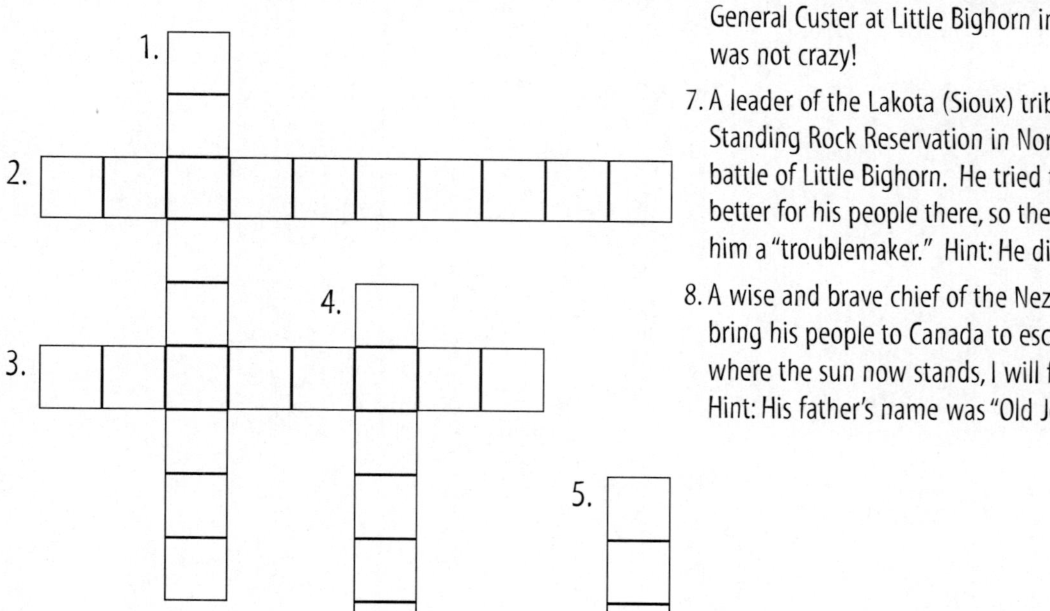

Answer Key: 1. Sacajawea; 2. Pocahontas; 3. Black Elk; 4. Sequoia; 5. Geronimo; 6. Crazy Horse; 7. Sitting Bull; 8. Chief Joseph

Different Ways for Different Indians!

North American Indian tribes are divided into different areas. In each of these areas, tribes shared common ways of living with each other. They might make similar arts or crafts, they might eat the same foods, or they might have had the same beliefs. These activities are all part of their "culture." Each area had its own culture, which was different from the tribes in all the other areas.

Below is a map of all the different groups of Indian tribes in North America. Color each area with a different color. You will see a colorful picture of how Native Americans can all be called "Indians" but still have very different cultures!

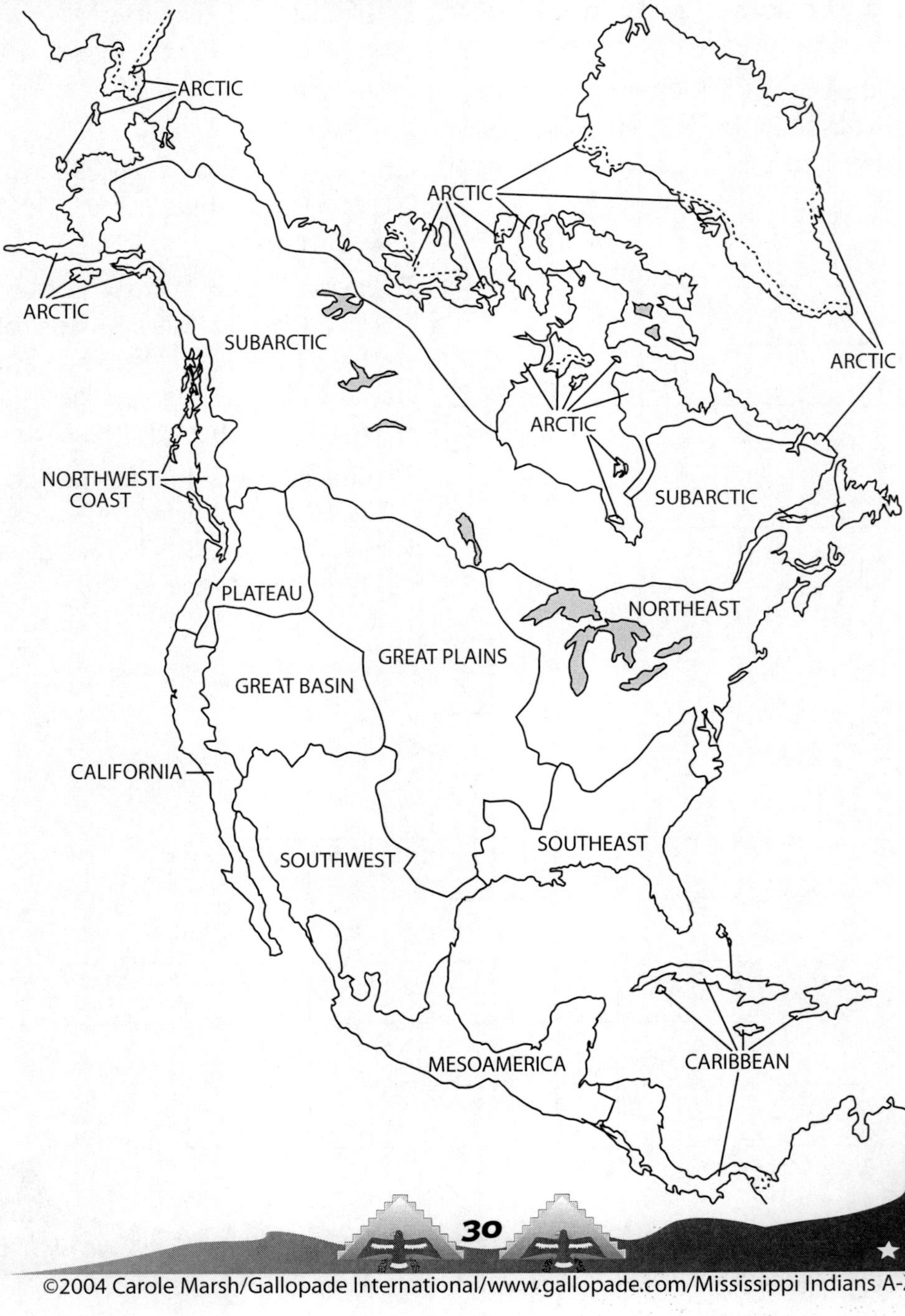

Celebration!

Powwows are big festivals where Native Americans gather to sing, dance, and eat together. It is a time to celebrate and show pride in their culture. Powwows can last from one afternoon to several days. The Indians dress in native costumes and dance ancient dances to the beating of drums.

Artists sell their arts and crafts. You might be able to buy some real Native American food cooked on an open fire. Native Americans go to powwows to be with each other, share ideas, and just have fun! Most powwows are also open to people who are not Indian. It's a great place to learn about Native American culture!

If you went to a powwow this weekend, what do you think you would see? What do you think might NOT be there? Circle the objects you think you would see at a powwow. Put an X through those you probably won't see.

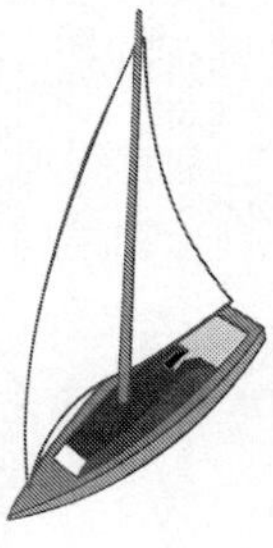

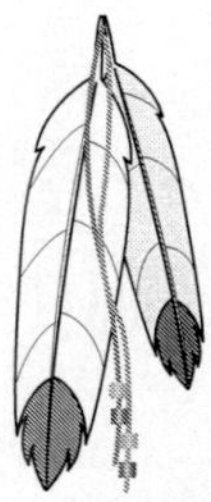

Answer Key: Circled objects are: beads, moccasins, open fire, drums, feathers, baskets, kids, food, drums, horse.

Make an Indian Weaving!

Many Native Americans used weaving to create useful things like sashes (belts), bags, mats, and blankets. They used animal hair to make yarn, and dyed the yarn with natural dyes from fruits and other plants. They also used some plant fibers, like cotton, to make weaving thread.

Weave a small Native American mat of your own. Use different colors of yarn to create a beautiful pattern in your weaving. Place a favorite object on the mat or hang it on your wall!

Prepare the "loom"

Cut a piece of cardboard 5 inches wide and 6 inches long. Along the two 5-inch sides (the "short" sides), have an adult cut slits 1/4 inch deep. These slits should be 1/2 inch apart from each other. So, on each short side you will have 9 slits.

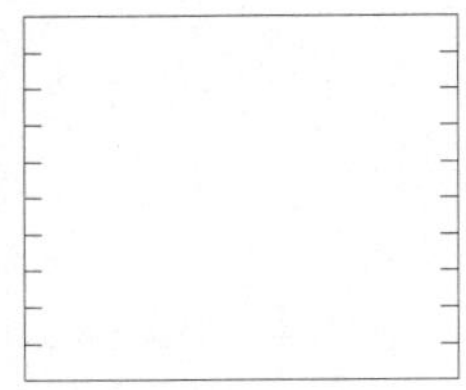

Directions:

1. Take a long piece of yarn and bring it from the back through the first slit (the one next to the edge of the cardboard.) The end of the yarn will hang down behind the cardboard.

2. Bring the yarn right across the front of the cardboard to the slit opposite the one your yarn came through.

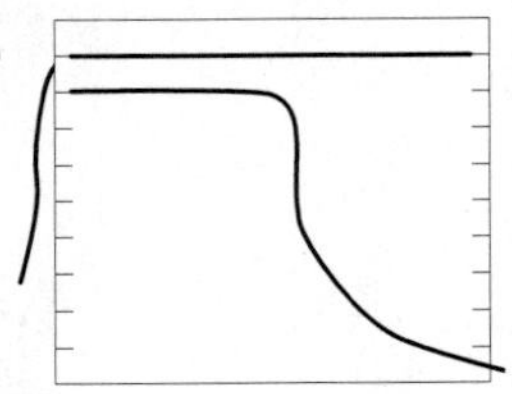

3. Now bring the yarn under the back of the cardboard and then up again through the second slit.

4. Repeat #2 and #3, until you have 9 strands of yarn across the front of your cardboard!

5. Then cut the yarn and tie the two loose ends in the back of the cardboard.

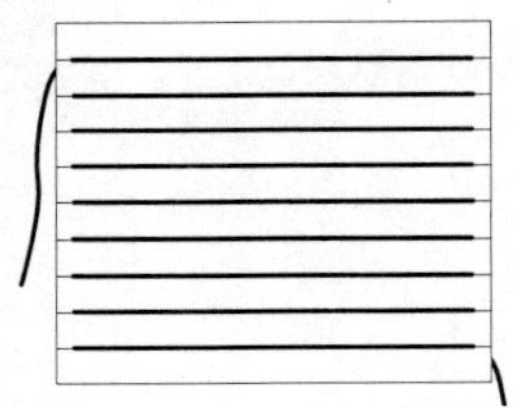

6. Take another piece of yarn and start feeding it through the 9 strands, going over one, under the next over the next, etc. When you get to the end, pull the yarn behind the cardboard and around to the front, and begin again. This time, whatever strand you went over, go under. And whatever strand you went under, go over.

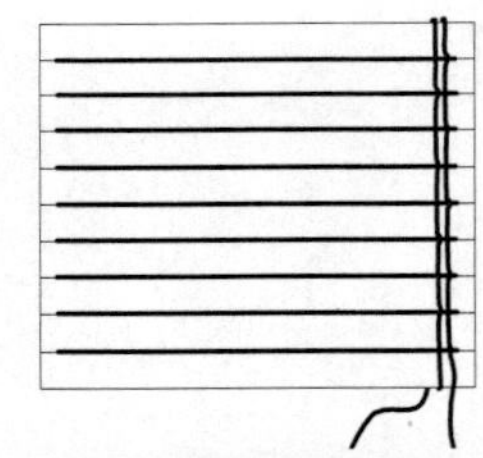

7. Repeat this pattern until the front of your cardboard in covered. Then cut the yarn in the back of the cardboard, and trim it to create a fringe for your mat!

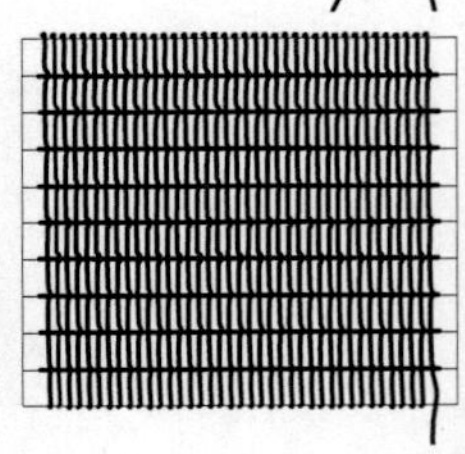

Tips!

- For a wild look, use variegated or different colored yarn!
- For a tighter mat, push the under/over strands up against the previous strands during weaving.
- To keep your mat from unravelling, tie neighboring fringe together up close to the mat.

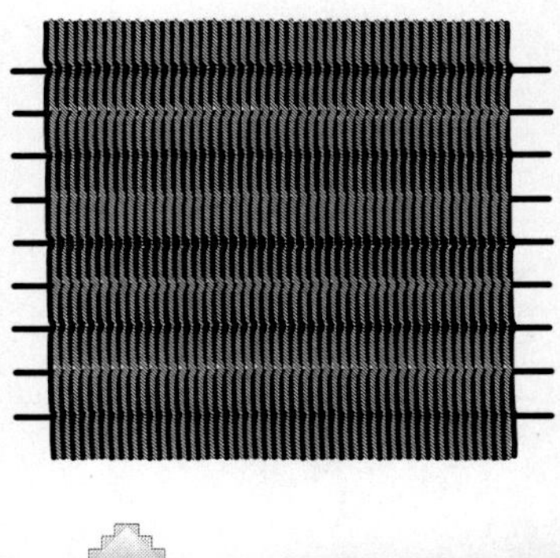

Finders Keepers?

Native Americans have many buried treasures. For hundreds of years, special objects would sometimes be buried with Native Americans, or maybe they would just be lost. Archeologists used to dig for interesting artifacts in old Native American gravesites. They would keep the Native American bones or the arrowheads, rattles, masks and other objects that they found. But this made the Native Americans feel like they were being robbed.

In 1990, the U.S. government passed a law that said that no one could look for or take these Native American objects anymore. And whoever had any already had to give them back to the people they belonged to. This is called repatriation

Help the archeologist return the artifact to a Native American.

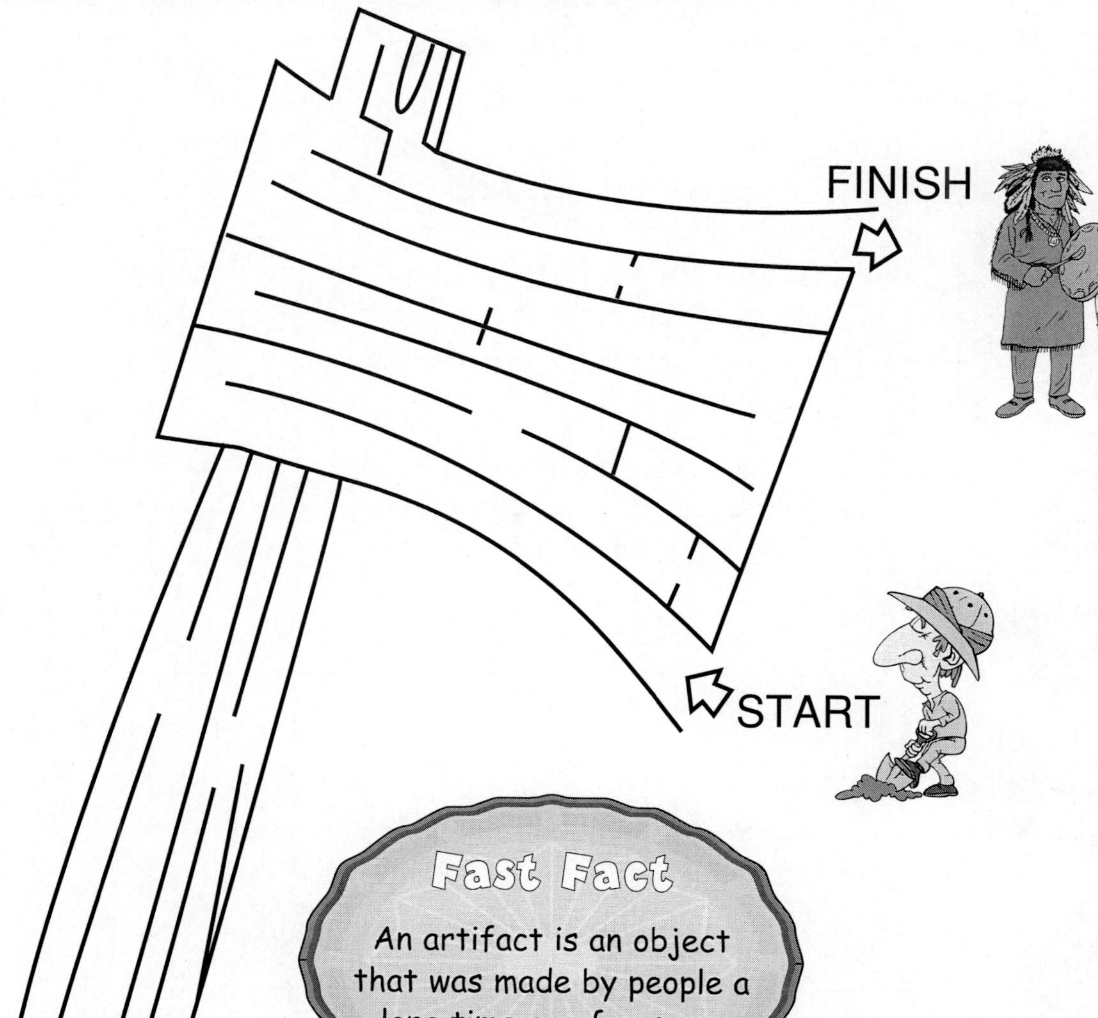

Fast Fact

An artifact is an object that was made by people a long time ago for some useful purpose.

Busy Hands!

Before modern times, Native Americans didn't have stores where they went to buy things. They made everything they needed.

What did Indians make with their own hands? Use the Word Bank and pictures to find out!

Word Bank

blanket	moccasins	arrows	pottery	canoe
mat	food	jewelry	pouch	box

___ ___ ___

___ ___ ___ ___

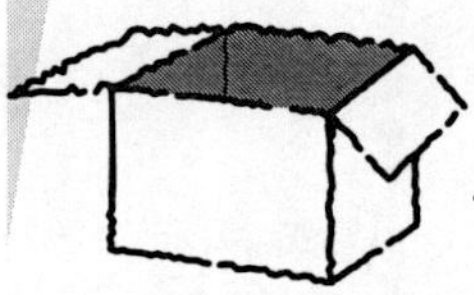

___ ___ ___

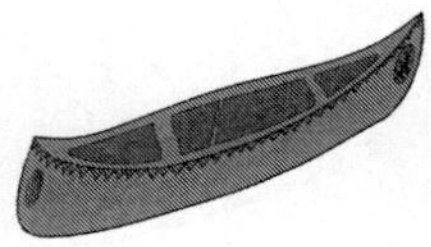

___ ___ ___ ___ ___ ___

___ ___ ___ ___ ___ ___ ___

___ ___ ___ ___ ___

___ ___ ___ ___ ___ ___ ___ ___ ___ ___

___ ___ ___ ___ ___ ___

___ ___ ___ ___ ___ ___ ___

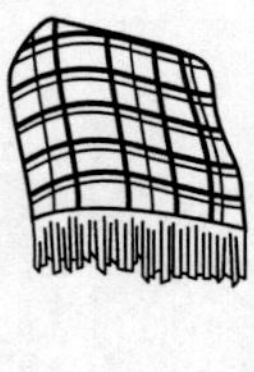

___ ___ ___ ___ ___ ___ ___

American Indians Today

Beginning with the first letter of each group of letters, cross out every other letter to discover some new words. You may not have heard of these before, but you can read all about them!

1. Many Indians live on these, but many more do not!

TRYELSDEBRNVJAOTPIPOWNASX

____

2. Many Indians have been poor for a long time because for many years the government took away their lands and their ability to make a living.

TPKOOVWEBRNTXYA

____

3. Many Indians have been studying hard at school and going to college in order to earn more money. Education helps the Indians make their lives better. These Native Americans are working to become:

TSJUMCBCFEYSMSOFPUVL

____

4. This is a big term that means Native Americans have worked hard to get the U.S. government to let them rule themselves. This means that they have their own laws and make their own decisions. They are like a separate country inside the U.S.! Now, try and see if you can get your parents to give you the same thing!

TSGENLBF **JDGEETSEWRAMCIHNUAKTYIKOTNU**

______________ ______________________________

Fast Fact

What do Indians work as today?

- doctors
- nurses
- factory workers
- artists
- lawyers
- actors

The same kinds of jobs any American might work at!

Native Americans Move to the City!

Solve the code to discover the mystery words!

A	B	C	D	E	F	G	H	I	J	K	L	M
✹	❁	✣	♣	➳	❤	❢	✲	✂	✆	☛	✈	✉
N	**O**	**P**	**Q**	**R**	**S**	**T**	**U**	**V**	**W**	**X**	**Y**	**Z**
✿	✩	✦	✡	✐	❦	☎	➽	✚	✖	✍	✠	✓

1. During the 1950s and 1960s, the American government paid Indians to leave their homes on reservations and move to cities to get jobs. If cities are sometimes called urban areas, then these brave Indians were called:

___ ___ ___ ___ ___   ___ ___ ___ ___ ___ ___ ___
➽ ✐ ❁ ✹ ✿   ✂ ✿ ♣ ✂ ✹ ✿ ❦

2. Many Indians chose to stay on their reservations and not move to the city. They thought that if they moved to the city, they would lose the way of life that their parents and ancestors had taught. These Indians called themselves:

___ ___ ___ ___ ___ ___ ___ ___ ___ ___ ___   ___ ___ ___ ___ ___ ___ ___
✐ ➳ ❦ ➳ ✐ ✚ ✹ ☎ ✂ ✩ ✿   ✂ ✿ ♣ ✂ ✹ ✿ ❦

3. Native Americans who moved to cities lived close to each other. They tried to keep their way of life as much as possible. They did not want to forget their religion, native art, or music. They did not want to lose their:

___ ___ ___ ___ ___ ___ ___
✣ ➽ ✈ ☎ ➽ ✐ ➳

4. Are you afraid of heights? Many people are. The Mohawk Indians are not! Many of them work hundreds of feet above the city to build steel frames for skyscrapers. People who do this work above the city are:

___ ___ ___ ___ ___   ___ ___ ___ ___ ___ ___ ___
❦ ☎ ➳ ➳ ✈   ✖ ✩ ✐ ☛ ➳ ✐ ❦

5. Today urban Indians and reservation Indians come together to celebrate their culture. They share ideas and stories. They dance and beat drums. They make and sell Indian jewelry. During these celebrations, Indians remember how much they have to be proud of! These big parties are called

___ ___ ___ ___ ___ ___ ___
✦ ✩ ✖ ✖ ✩ ✖ ❦